U0132316

*Isn't it great to see a friend
from afar?*

有朋自遠方來，不亦樂乎？

學而 1

Developing new ideas out of old knowledge makes a teacher.

溫故而知新，可以為師矣。

為政 11

The superior man knows righteousness; the inferior man knows self-gain.

君子喻於義，小人喻於利。

里仁 16

The superior man unites with people yet not plot with them; the inferior man plots with people yet not unite with them.

君子周而不比，小人比而不周。

為政 14

Learning without thought
will be confusing.
Thinking without learning
will be dangerous.

學而不思則罔，思而不學則殆。

為政 15

Say yes if you know.
Say no if you don't.
That is the point.

知之為知之，不知為不知，是知也。

為政 17

Do you know?

Confucius's father named him Qiu,
literally meaning hills, for his head was
shaped like hills surrounding a piece of
concave land.

孔父為孔子取名為丘，
是因為他頭頂中間凹陷，
四邊卻凸起如山丘。

When meeting a virtuous man,
one should learn to be like him;
when meeting a non-virtuous man,
one should examine oneself.

見賢思齊焉，見不賢而內自省也。

里仁 17

While your parents are alive, you should not travel afar. If it is a must to travel, your whereabouts should be known.

父母在，不遠遊。遊必有方。

里仁 19

In the past people will choose not to speak for the fear that they cannot act upon their words. Breaking one's promise makes one feel ashamed.

古者言之不出，恥躬之不逮也。

里仁 22

The superior man wishes to speak slowly but act promptly.

君子欲訥於言，而敏於行。

里仁 24

Understanding a person requires analysing one's motives, observing one's actions and understanding one's attitude.

視其所以，觀其所由，察其所安。

為政 10

One cannot endure prolonged poverty nor appreciate happiness if one is not humane.

不仁者不可以久處約，不可以長處樂。

里仁 2

In the morning could I learn the Way, I would die content in the evening.

朝聞道，夕死可矣。

里仁 8

Do you know?

Confucius was famous for
being tall (around 190cm) and
nicknamed "Long Man" in *Records of
the Grand Historian.*

孔子是著名的高個子，
更在《史記》中被稱為"長人"呢：
"孔子長九尺有六寸，
人皆謂之'長人'而異之。"

The 300 poems in the Book of Poetry can be summed up in one phrase: thoughts not diverted from the Way.

詩三百，一言以蔽之，曰"思無邪"。

為政 2

Education for all.

有教無類。

衛靈公 39

A humane man finds peace in humanity. A wise man finds benefits in humanity.

仁者安仁，知者利仁。

里仁 2

One should aim at the Way, base oneself on virtue, lean on humanity and take pleasure in the arts.

志於道，據於德，依於仁，游於藝。

述而 6

You cannot reach your goal in haste, and you cannot achieve great things if you covet petty gains.

欲速，則不達；見小利，則大事不成。

子路 17

The superior man is concerned about the law; the inferior man about favours.

君子懷刑，小人懷惠。

里仁 11

One should not worry about not being offered any official position, but about not being qualified.

不患無位，患所以立。

里仁 14

Do you know?

Confucius was quite a traveller:
he spent 14 years travelling around to
find a feudal state, such as Wei,
Cai and Chen, to accept his ideas.

孔子可算是一位旅行家，
曾周遊列國 14 年，到訪衛、蔡、
陳等國希望政見獲接納。

One should not worry about not being understood, but not understanding others.

不患人之不己知，患不知人也。

學而 16

How can an untrustworthy man do anything?

人而無信，不知其可也。

為政 22

One should not seek to be well-known, but seek to be worth knowing for genuine qualities.

不患莫己知，求為可知也。

里仁 14

To know the Way is not so good as to like it; to like it is not so good as to rejoice in it.

知之者不如好之者，好之者不如樂之者。

雍也 20

The wise like water,
the humane like mountains.

知者樂水，仁者樂山。

雍也 23

A superior man who learns the classics and abides by the ritual will not deviate from the Way.

君子博學於文，約之以禮，亦可以弗畔矣夫！

雍也 27、顏淵 15

Do you know?

Confucius is multi-talented and good at the Six Arts: archery, charioting, music, ritual, mathematics, calligraphy.

孔子並非羸弱書生，
更精於禮、樂、射、御、書、數，
合稱六藝。

The Mean is the greatest of all the virtues. The ordinary people lack it for a long time.

中庸之為德也，其至矣乎！民鮮久矣。

雍也 29

I am not those who are born with knowledge, but I love studying classics and seeking knowledge.

我非生而知之者，好古，敏以求之者也。

述而 20

The wise are active;
the humane are quiet.

知者動，仁者靜。

雍也 23

Only in severe cold does one know that the pine and the cypress are the last to wither.

歲寒，然後知松柏之後凋也。

子罕 28

The wise are happy;
the humane enjoys longevity.

知者樂，仁者壽。

雍也 23

Learn knowledge at heart, study continuously and teach others tirelessly—can any of them be difficult to me?

默而識之，學而不厭，誨人不倦，
何有於我哉？

述而 2

When at home, young people should be obedient; when away from home, they should be respectful and honest, love others and get close to kind people.

弟子入則孝，出則弟，謹而信，泛愛眾，而親仁。

學而 6

Do you know?

Confucius was married at 19.
It was said that Confucius, his son and
grandson divorced their wives.

孔子十九歲時結婚，
據記載孔門三代皆休妻。

If a superior man lacks solemnity,
he will not be awe-inspiring;
if he is willing to learn,
he will not be rigid.

君子不重則不威，學則不固。

學而 8

A superior man does not get himself stuffed or look for a comfortable home. He is smart in his work and careful in his speech; he goes to people knowledgeable of the Way and corrects his mistakes.

君子食無求飽，居無求安，敏於事而慎於言，
就有道而正焉……。

學而 14

42

People make typical mistakes of their own. You can understand a person by observing one's errors.

人之過也，各於其黨。觀過，斯知仁矣。

里仁 7

Do you know?

Confucius did various jobs to earn a living, including shepherd and stable manager.

孔子為了養家做過很多工作，
例如牧養牲口、管理倉儲。

"Shen, my Way is bound by one single thread," Confucius said to Zeng Shen. Then a disciple asked, "What does it mean?" Zeng answered, "Confucius's Way is to be loyal and forgiving, and that's it."

參乎，吾道一以貫之。⋯⋯門人問曰：何謂也？
曾夫子之道，忠恕而已矣。

里仁 15

Confucius thought Zi Chan had four characteristics of a superior man: he behaves properly with courtesy, he serves his superiors with deep respect, he is caring for the people and he treats them fairly.

子謂子產，有君子之道四焉：其行己也恭，
其事上也敬，其養民也惠，其使民也義。

公冶長 16

Bo Yi and Shu Qi did not
bear old grudges against others,
therefore little resentment was held
against them.

伯夷、叔齊不念舊惡，怨是用希。

公冶長 23

Sly words, fawning faces and subservience to others… Being friendly to someone whom you secretly hold a grudge against— Zuo found it shameful, I also found it shameful.

巧言、令色、足恭……匿怨而友其人，
左丘明恥之，丘亦恥之。

公冶長 25

Yan Hui is indeed a virtuous man! A small bamboo basket of rice, a gourd-ladle of water and a shabby home—people would find such living conditions intolerable but Hui enjoyed them.

賢哉回也！一簞食，一瓢飲，在陋巷。
人不堪其憂，回也不改其樂。

雍也 11

That people can survive is because of their uprightness. If a person survives without being upright, then it is because he barely escapes from misfortune.

人之生也直，罔之生也幸而免。

雍也 19

Not cultivating one's virtue, not digging into the knowledge that has been learnt, not following others' good deeds and not correcting one's mistakes: these are the things that worry me.

德之不脩，學之不講，聞義不能徙，不善不能改，是吾憂也。

述而 3

A superior man upholds the importance of loyalty, has no friends not as good as himself and does not hesitate to correct his own mistakes.

主忠信，無友不如己者，過則勿憚改。

學而 8

Do you know?

The highest position that Confucius
held was the Minister of Crime.

孔子做過最高的官位是"司寇",
相當於現今的最高法官。

Eating coarse food, drinking water and sleeping with a bent elbow as a pillow make me happy. Wealth and nobility gained in an immoral way are like floating clouds to me.

飯疏食飲水，曲肱而枕之，樂亦在其中矣。
不義而富且貴，於我如浮雲。

述而 16

I do not talk about monsters, force, rebellion, ghosts or gods.

子不語怪，力，亂，神。

述而 21

If I am walking with two other men, I can often find teachers in them. I will choose to learn his good qualities and correct the similar bad qualities in myself.

三人行，必有我師焉。擇其善者而從之，
其不善者而改之。

述而 22

Confucius taught four kinds of subjects: the classics, social practice, loyalty and trustworthiness.

子以四教：文，行，忠，信。

述而 25

I listen to opinions widely and choose the good ones to follow. I also observe broadly and make sense of my observation. This would be the second level of attaining knowledge.

多聞擇其善者而從之，多見而識之，知之次也。

述而 28

Luxury means lack of self-discipline. Frugality means rigidity. I would rather be rigid than being undisciplined.

奢則不孫，儉則固。與其不孫也，寧固。

述而 36

The superior man is frank and at ease while the inferior man is full of worries and anxieties.

君子坦蕩蕩，小人長戚戚。

述而 37

Do you know?

Confucius was the first Chinese
to set up a private school admitting
students from all walks of life.
At that time, only aristocrats could
receive education.

孔子是中國首位辦私學的老師，
接受來自各階層的學生，
而周代只有貴族可以唸書。

Confucius was mild yet solemn, awe-inspiring but not fearsome, dignified but peaceful.

子溫而厲，威而不猛，恭而安。

述而 38

One will be inspired by poetry, able to establish oneself by ritual and cultivated by music.

興於詩，立於禮，成於樂。

泰伯 8

I cannot understand people who are arrogant but not upright, simple-minded yet dishonest, seemingly genuine yet unable to keep a promise.

狂而不直，侗而不愿，悾悾而不信，吾不知之矣。

泰伯 16

Learn as if you are going to fall behind, and continue to learn as if you might lose what you have learned.

學如不及，猶恐失之。

泰伯 17

*Confucius refuses four kinds
of behaviours: groundless
speculation, insistence on certainty,
inflexibility and egotism.*

子絕四：毋意，毋必，毋固，毋我。

子罕 4

Confucius said by the river bank,
"What elapses is like the flowing
river! Day or night it will never
cease."

子在川上，曰：逝者如斯夫！不舍晝夜。

子罕 17

Do you know?

Confucius has many disciples of various talents. The most outstanding ten are:

Virtues: Yan Yuan, Min Ziqian,
Ran Boniu, Zhong Gong
Language: Zai Wo, Zi Gong
Politics: Ran You, Ji Lu
Literature: Zi You, Zi Xia

孔子的學生各有所長，
當中最出色的是孔門十哲：

德行：顏淵、閔子騫、冉伯牛、仲弓；
言語：宰我、子貢；
政事：冉有、季路；
文學：子游、子夏。

Confucius said, "There are sprouts that do not blossom, and there are blossoms that do not bear fruit."

子曰：苗而不秀者有矣夫！
秀而不實者有矣夫！

子罕 22

*Am I knowledgeable? No, when
I was asked by an uncultured
man, I couldn't answer his
questions at all. Then I kept
asking him questions between pros
and cons and finally the doubts
were all cleared.*

吾有知乎哉？無知也。有鄙夫問於我，
空空如也，我叩其兩端而竭焉。

子罕 8

The general of the three armed services might be seized, but a man's will cannot be taken away.

三軍可奪帥也，匹夫不可奪志也。

子罕 25

One who is wise will not be confused. One who is humane will not worry. One who is courageous will not be afraid.

知者不惑，仁者不憂，勇者不懼。

子罕 29

Do not make plans of government affairs unless they are within the responsibilities of your position.

不在其位，不謀其政。

憲問 26

"Zi Zhang always goes too far, while Zi Xia is not enough." Zi Gong asked, *"So is Zi Zhang better?"* Confucius answered, *"Going too far is just as bad as being not enough."*

師也過，商也不及。曰：然則師愈與？過猶不及。

先進 16

Zi Zhang asked about the Way of being a virtuous man. Confucius said, "A virtuous man does not show his trace of doing good deeds or confine himself to the thought of doing good deeds."

子張問善人之道。不踐跡，亦不入於室。

先進 20

Do you know?

Confucius said he had been studying diligently since 15, and had established his lifelong goals at 30.

談到自己，孔子說"十有五而志於學，三十而立"，"立"不是指成家立室，而是建立明確的人生方向。

Zi Zhang asked about politics. Confucius answered, "Never show weariness in your work. Carry out your duties loyally."

子張問政。居之無倦，行之以忠。

顏淵 14

The superior man helps others to develop what is good while the inferior man does the opposite.

君子成人之美，不成人之惡。小人反是。

顏淵 16

*Give good advice to lead your
friends to the Way. If they do not
accept it, stop giving advice.
Do not disgrace yourself.*

忠告而善道之，不可則止，無自辱焉。

顏淵 23

Zi Lu asked about politics.
Confucius said, "Act as an
example for your subordinates and
urge them to work hard."
Zi Lu asked him to talk more.
He answered, "Never slack off."

子路問政。先之，勞之。請益。曰：無倦。

子路 1

Do you know?

Confucius spoke highly of
Zhou Gong Dan, a devoted regent of the
Zhou Dynasty, and often dreamt of him.
Thus "meeting Zhou Gong" has
become a popular saying which now
refers to going to sleep or dreaming.

孔子十分推崇周公旦，還因為日有所思，
夜有所夢，經常夢到周公，
後人便以"夢周公"代指睡覺、做夢。

An upright man is obeyed even if he gives no orders while a man who is not upright is not obeyed even if he gives orders.

其身正，不令而行；其身不正，雖令不從。

子路 6

Act properly at home, work with a respectful attitude and be loyal to others. Obey the above principles even when you go to places where barbarians live.

居處恭，執事敬，與人忠。
雖之夷狄，不可棄也。

子路 19

The superior man aims at harmony, not at uniformity while the inferior man the other way round.

君子和而不同，小人同而不和。

子路 23

The superior man is confident but not arrogant while the inferior man is arrogant but cowardly .

君子泰而不驕，小人驕而不泰。

子路 26

The firm, the persistent, the simple and the reticent people are near to humaneness.

剛、毅、木、訥，近仁。

子路 27

Virtuous people are always ready to speak but talkative people might not be virtuous. The humane are always brave but brave men might not be humane.

有德者，必有言。有言者，不必有德。
仁者，必有勇。勇者，不必有仁。

憲問 4

There are superior men who are not virtuous but there are no inferior men who are virtuous.

君子而不仁者有矣夫，未有小人而仁者也。

憲問 6

How can you love a person without making sacrifice? How can you be loyal to people without offering them advice?

愛之，能勿勞乎？忠焉，能勿誨乎？

憲問 7

It is difficult to be poor without complaining but easy to be rich without being arrogant.

貧而無怨難，富而無驕易。

憲問 10

If your words are arrogant,
it will be difficult to achieve
what you have said.

其言之不怍，則為之也難。

憲問 20

Do you know?

Many Chinese idioms coming from
The Analects are still in use today,
such as "to emulate people
who are better than oneself".

不少常見的成語來自《論語》，
例如"見賢思齊"。

The superior man goes to up above while the inferior man goes to down below.

君子上達，小人下達。

憲問 23

A superior man does not think beyond his duties.

君子思不出其位。

憲問 26

The superior man thinks that
it is a shame to talk
more than he does.

君子恥其言而過其行。

憲問 27

The humane ones do not worry, the wise ones do not feel confused and the brave ones do not fear.

君子道者三，我無能焉：仁者不憂，知者不惑，
勇者不懼。子貢曰：夫子自道也。

憲問 28

*Do not be bothered by others'
lack of understanding about one's
abilities, but by one's own lack of
abilities.*

不患人之不己知，患其不能也。

憲問 30

If one who does not anticipate being deceived or presume disloyalty from others can still detect such behaviours, shouldn't such a man be called superior?

不逆詐，不億不信。抑亦先覺者，是賢乎！

憲問 31

The worth of an excellent horse lies not in its strength but its virtue.

驥不稱其力，稱其德也。

憲問 33

To repay others' menace
with uprightness, and virtues
with virtues.

以直報怨，以德報德。

憲問 34

Do you know?

Confucius was titled "Zhong Ni",
named after Mount Zhongni in Qufu
where he was born. In ancient Chinese,
Zhong means the second child while Bo
means the first child.
That is why Confucius's elder brother
was titled "Bo Ni".

孔子的出生地曲阜有一座尼山，
本稱尼丘山，孔子名字裏的"丘"和"尼"
都和出生地有關。傳統會用"伯"表示最
大的兒子，"仲"表示排行第二，
而孔子的確有一個同父異母的哥哥，
他的名字就是伯尼。

If you do not talk to people with whom you can talk to, you will lose them; if you talk to people with whom you should not, you are saying the wrong words.

可與言而不與之言，失人；
不可與言而與之言，失言。

衛靈公 8

A virtuous, benevolent person will not compromise benevolence for his survival; he will sacrifice himself for the sake of benevolence.

志士仁人，無求生以害仁，有殺身以成仁。

衛靈公 9

A craftsman sharpens his tools to make the perfect product. When one lives in a certain place, one should follow officials of wisdom and get along with friends of benevolence.

工欲善其事，必先利其器。居是邦也，事其大夫之賢者，友其士之仁者。

衛靈公 10

A person with no future plans must have impending worries.

人無遠慮，必有近憂。

衛靈公 12

One can avoid hatred by blaming oneself rather than accusing others.

躬自厚而薄責於人，則遠怨矣。

衛靈公 15

If one always hangs around with the inferior man, one will not talk about justice but play petty tricks. It is difficult to deal with people like this.

群居終日，言不及義，好行小慧，難矣哉！

衛靈公 17

The superior man upholds justice as essence, practise ritual in his daily behaviours and show humbleness in his speech and loyalty in self-development.

君子義以為質，禮以行之，孫以出之，信以成之。

衛靈公 18

A superior man worries about his own inability, not others' inability to know about himself.

君子病無能焉，不病人之不己知也。

衛靈公 19

Do you know?

Once Confucius got lost and while his
disciples were searching for him,
a passer-by said a man who looked like
a stray dog was standing by the gate.
When Confucius knew it later,
he gave a laugh and agreed with the
passer-by's comment!

有一次孔子和弟子走失，
弟子問路時途人說在城門附近看到一個
喪家犬似的人站着，孔子知道後竟自嘲
的確有點像喪家犬呢！

*The superior man worries that
their names are not remembered or
spread after death.*

君子疾沒世而名不稱焉。

衛靈公 20

The superior man seeks all from himself while the inferior man seeks all from others.

君子求諸己，小人求諸人。

衛靈公 21

The superior man treats highly of himself and does not want to fight, has friends but does not form circles.

君子矜而不爭，群而不黨。

衛靈公 22

The superior man does not recommend a person just because of what he says, nor does he ignore what a person says because of his shortcomings.

君子不以言舉人，不以人廢言。

衛靈公 23

*Do not impose on others
what you do not desire
yourself.*

己所不欲，勿施於人。

衛靈公 24

Sly words disturb virtues.
Not restraining one's temper
on trivialities disturb great
plans.

巧言亂德，小不忍則亂大謀。

衛靈公 27

*What everyone hates should
be carefully researched; what
everyone likes must also be
carefully researched.*

眾惡之，必察焉；眾好之，必察焉。

衛靈公 28

A mistake remains
uncorrected is a real mistake.

過而不改，是謂過矣。

衛靈公 30

Do you know?

The Confucian Temple in Confucius's hometown, Qufu of Shandong Province, was reserved well even during the Second World War.

位於孔子故鄉（山東曲阜）的孔廟，
即使在二戰期間，也保存完整。

*I tried spending a whole day
not eating and a whole night not
sleeping to think. It ended fruitless
that I should have studied instead
of making mere thoughts.*

吾嘗終日不食，終夜不寢，以思，
無益，不如學也。

衛靈公 31

Do not give way to even your teachers when it comes to the practice of humaneness.

當仁不讓於師。

衛靈公 36

The superior man remains steadfast without being rigid.

君子貞而不諒。

衛靈公 37

When serving the superiors, focus on the service itself before thinking about your payoffs.

事君，敬其事而後其食。

衛靈公 38

Do not discuss with people with diverting paths from yours.

道不同，不相為謀。

衛靈公 40

The superior man fears three things: the will of Heaven, men of high rank and the words of the sages.

君子有三畏：畏天命，畏大人，畏聖人之言。

季氏 8

The inferior man does not know of the will of Heaven and thus has no reverence for it. He does not respect men of high rank and thus ridicules the words of the sages.

小人不知天命而不畏也，狎大人，侮聖人之言。

季氏 8

Men are similar to one another by nature, yet different due to learning and practice.

性相近也，習相遠也。

陽貨 2

Do you know?

The Confucius family tree, started in the Spring and Autumn Period, is the longest recorded pedigree in the world. It is recorded that Confucius has 2 million registered descendants.

春秋時代開始的《孔子世家譜》是世界上最長的家譜，記錄孔氏家族達 2 百萬人！

*A coward wearing a stern face is
no difference to an inferior man or
a burglar who climbs over walls
to steal.*

色厲而內荏，譬諸小人，其猶穿窬之盜也與？

陽貨 12

Those who believe in hearsay cast away their virtues.

道聽而塗説，德之棄也。

陽貨 14

These men are so mean! …They are worried about not getting what they desire, and when they have got it, they are worried about losing it. They are always worrying, and there is nothing that doesn't worry them.

鄙夫！……其未得之也，患得之；既得之，患失之。苟患失之，無所不至矣。

陽貨 15

*How hard it is to have a full belly
and an absent mind all the time?
Isn't there a thing called chess?
Even playing chess is better than
doing nothing.*

飽食終日，無所用心，難矣哉！不有博弈者乎，
為之猶賢乎已。

陽貨 22

The superior man upholds justice.
A brave superior man lacking
justice will cause disturbance; a
brave inferior man lacking justice
will become a thief.

君子義以為上。君子有勇而無義為亂，
小人有勇而無義為盜。

陽貨 23

Do you know?

There are 500 Confucius Institutes all over the world. One of them was even opened in a prison in 2016 where students receive traditional teaching of calligraphy, reading classics and moral cultivation.

以孔子命名的 "孔子學院"
在全球共有 500 所，2016 年更在監獄開校，
學員會接受書法、
讀經和道德課等傳統教育。

It is difficult to get along with women and the inferior man. If you get too close to them, they will lose manners; if you stay away from them, they will bear a grudge.

唯女子與小人為難養也，近之則不孫，
遠之則怨。

陽貨 25

One who does not understand fate cannot be a superior man. One who does not understand the ritual cannot be established. One who does not understand words cannot understand people.

不知命，無以為君子也。不知禮，無以立也。
不知言，無以知人也。

堯曰 3

Confucius's Works and Key Terms

重要著作及關鍵字

詩經　　　The Book of Odes

書經　　　The Book of Changes

易經　　　The Book of Documents

禮經　　　The Book of Rites

樂經　　　The Book of Music

春秋經　　Spring and Autumn Annals

論語　　　The Analects

仁　　　　humaneness, benevolence

義　　　　righteousness, fairness, justice

禮　　　　propriety, ritual

智　　　　moral wisdom

忠　　　　loyalty

信　　　　trustworthiness

孝　　　　filial piety

中庸　　　the Mean, the state of equilibrium and harmony